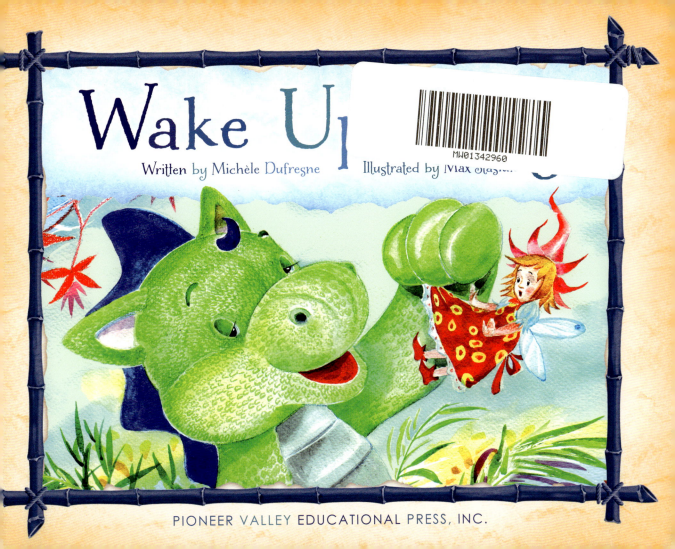

Wake Up

Written by Michèle Dufresne   Illustrated by Max ...

PIONEER VALLEY EDUCATIONAL PRESS, INC.

Here is a fairy.

The fairy is asleep.

Here is Clarence.

Clarence is hungry.

"Look," said Clarence.

"Berries! Yum! Yum! Yum!

I like berries."

"Look," said Clarence.

"Yum! Bananas!

I like bananas."

"Look," said Clarence.

"Coconuts! Yum! Yum! Yum! I like coconuts."

"Look, a bug!"
said Clarence.
"Yum! Yum!
I like bugs."

"Oh, no!" said the fairy.

"No! No! No!"

Here is the fairy.

The fairy is riding on Clarence.

The fairy is safe!

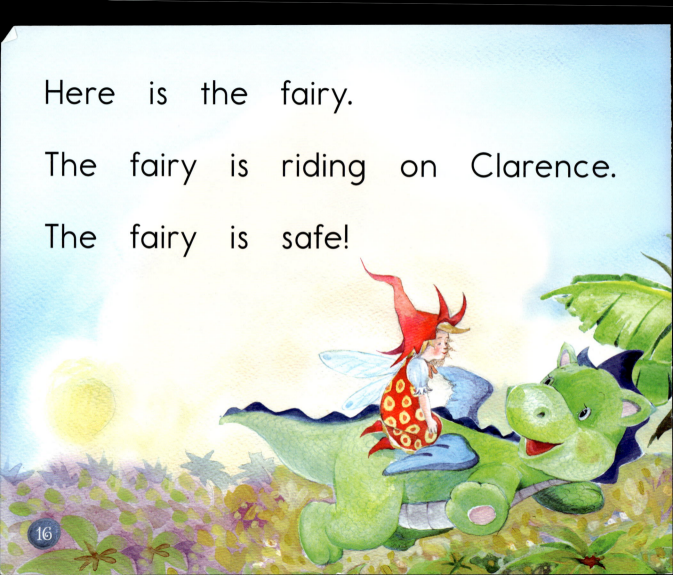